How to
GET YOUR TEACHER READY

How to GET YOUR TEACHER READY

by Jean Reagan
illustrated by Lee Wildish

DRAGONFLY BOOKS  NEW YORK

For teachers everywhere. You are truly amazing.

—J.R.

Text copyright © 2017 by Jean Reagan
Cover art and interior illustrations copyright © 2017 by Lee Wildish

Visit us on the Web! rhcbooks.com

Educators and librarians, for a variety of teaching tools, visit us at
RHTeachersLibrarians.com

Library of Congress Cataloging-in-Publication Data is available upon request.
ISBN 978-0-553-53825-0 (trade) — ISBN 978-0-553-53826-7 (lib. bdg.)
ISBN 978-0-553-53827-4 (ebook) — ISBN 978-0-593-30193-7 (pbk.)

MANUFACTURED IN CHINA
10 9 8 7 6 5 4 3 2

First Dragonfly Books Edition

You're ready for the first day of school.
But what about your teacher?

Make her feel welcome with
an extra-big smile. Then . . .

HOW TO WELCOME YOUR TEACHER:

⭐ Sing a "Good morning" song!

⭐ Show her your favorite spots in the room.

If she asks, "Why don't I have a cubby?" point to all the drawers in her very own desk.

Whisper, "I know where the bathroom is, if you ever need to go."

BATHROOM
→

School days are busy, so make sure she's ready for . . .

⭐ Art—Button up her smock *before* a disaster.

⭐ Lunch—Share your secret: "You get extra spaghetti if you *say* please."

⭐ Library time— Show her where to find the iguana books.

When it's time to go home, tell your teacher,
"Good job today! Ready for tomorrow?"

As the year gets going, there are lots of special things to get ready for. Like . . .

PICTURE DAY . . .

✦ Remind your teacher, "No messy snacks."

Chocolate cupcakes? Nope!

Powdered donuts? Nope!

Juicy, juicy pomegranates?

Nope!

✦ Take a look at her hair. Does she need a comb?

⭐ Then, instead of saying, "Cheeeeeeese!" say, "Teeeeeeeeeeeeacher!"

Perfect!
Now it's time for messy snacks.

... or a HOLIDAY CONCERT...

If your teacher's feeling nervous, show her how to *tiptoe*, *tiptoe*, *tiptoe* to the side of the curtain. Pull it back a teeny bit. Once she spots her family, she'll be ready to "La la la!"

. . . or *THE 100TH DAY OF SCHOOL.*

Everyone get ready to:

⭐ Jump up and down 100 times.

⭐ Plant 100 bulbs.

⭐ Count 100 toes.

⭐ And if you still have time, tell 100 jokes.

Some days—even when your teacher is ready—
things don't work out as planned:

★ The class pet escapes.

★ All the planets crash down
as the principal pops in.

★ Or rain ruins everything.

How can you help? Quick—hand her a favorite book!

When the day *finally* ends, say, "Don't worry.
Tomorrow we'll *all* be ready for a brand-new day."

Your teacher knows a lot, but not *everything*!
So ask, "Are you ready to be . . . amazed?"

THEN TEACH HER ALL ABOUT:

⋆ Big, stinky flowers of
   the jungle.

⋆ What elephants, naked
   mole rats, hummingbirds,
   and Venus flytraps
   like to eat.

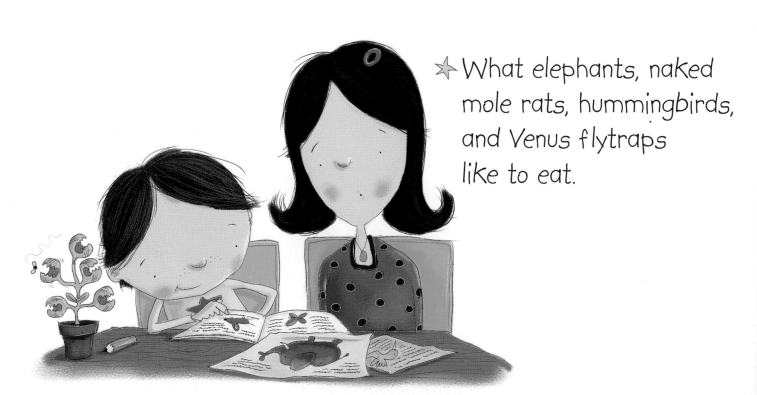

⭐ The sounds of a howler monkey.

"GAHOO!

GAHOO!

GAHOO!"

⭐ How sometimes magic—happens—very—slowly.

When spring comes, it's time for Field Day!

HOW TO GET YOUR TEACHER READY FOR FIELD DAY:

★ Make sure her whistle works.

✩ Help pick out her fastest shoes. Double-knot the laces.

✩ Does she have her water?
Her hat?
Her sunscreen?

Now everyone shout, "READY, SET . . ."

"...GOOOOOOOO!"

On Teacher Appreciation Day, you don't want your teacher to be *ready*. You want her to be . . . *surprised*.

HOW TO CELEBRATE YOUR TEACHER:

✫ Everyone dress in her favorite color.

✫ Say "teacher" in all the languages your class knows.

⭐ Give her something special, but definitely not . . . .
A big, stinky jungle flower.
An ice sculpture for her desk.
An already-opened box of chocolates.

As the year ends, get your teacher ready for one last thing . . . *goodbye.*

HOW TO SAY GOODBYE TO YOUR TEACHER:

⭐ Decorate a thank-you card with all the things you learned.

⭐ Surround her for a whole-class hug.

⭐ Give her one last extra-big smile.

Now your teacher's ready for a new class.
You're ready, too, for a whole new year. But . . .

Your teacher will remember you forever.
And you'll remember her.

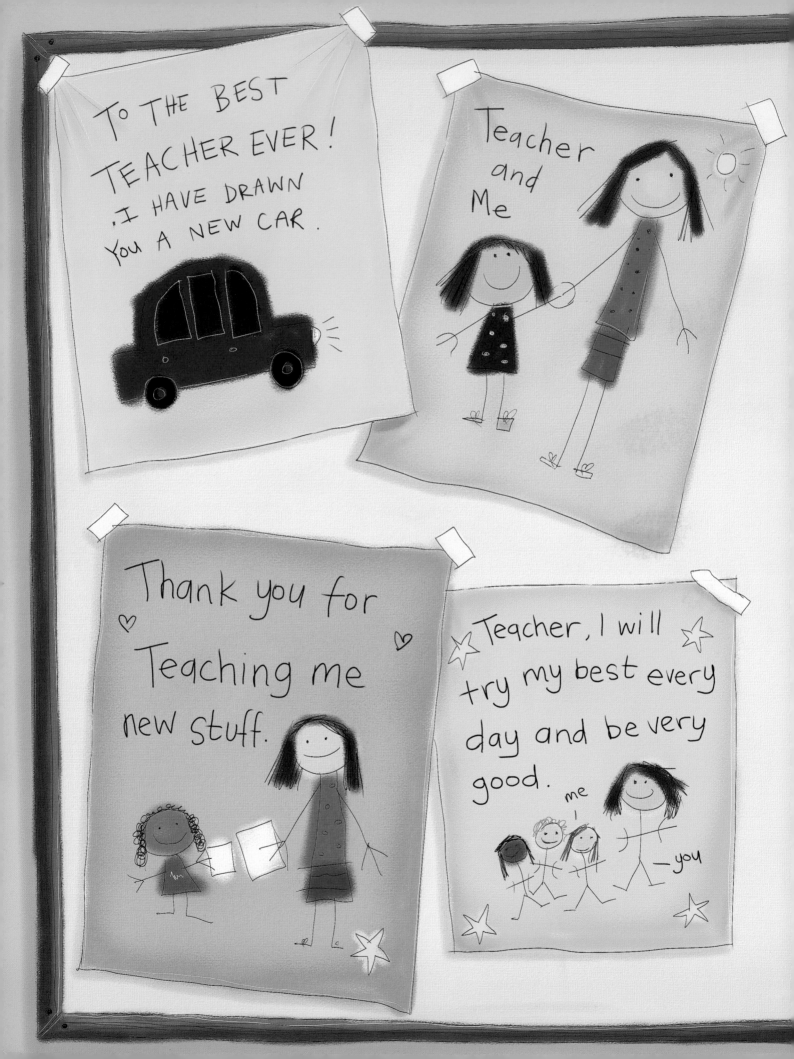

You are my favorite Teacher ever!

I don't have a gift,

but I drew an apple to give to you.

I like it when we play and you teach me new things.

To the best Teacher,

your lessons are the best.